FLAMINGO BINGO

By Heidi E. Y. Stemple

Illustrated by Aaron Spurgeon

Ready-to-Read

Simon Spotlight
New York   London   Toronto   Sydney   New Delhi

For my Dodo Bingo Crew: Lila,
Reese, Hazel, Nathan, Alex, Nate,
Sammy, and Jem.
—H. E. Y. S.

SIMON SPOTLIGHT

An imprint of Simon & Schuster Children's Publishing Division

1230 Avenue of the Americas, New York, New York 10020

This Simon Spotlight edition May 2022

Text copyright © 2022 by Heidi E. Y. Stemple

Illustrations copyright © 2022 by Aaron Spurgeon

SIMON SPOTLIGHT, READY-TO-READ, and colophon are registered trademarks of Simon & Schuster, Inc.

For information about special discounts for bulk purchases, please contact Simon & Schuster Special Sales at 1-866-506-1949 or business@simonandschuster.com.

Manufactured in the United States of America 0322 LAK

10 9 8 7 6 5 4 3 2 1

Library of Congress Cataloging-in-Publication Data

Names: Stemple, Heidi E.Y., author. | Spurgeon, Aaron, illustrator.

Title: Flamingo bingo / by Heidi E. Y. Stemple ; illustrated by Aaron Spurgeon.

Description: Simon Spotlight edition. | New York : Simon Spotlight, [2022]

Series: Ready-to-read | Summary: Birds of different feathers play bingo together, and watch the balls spin as they all hope to win.

Identifiers: LCCN 2021041115 | ISBN 9781665913867 (paperback)

ISBN 9781665913874 (hardcover) | ISBN 9781665913881 (ebook)

Subjects: CYAC: Stories in rhyme. | Flamingos—Fiction. | Birds—Fiction. | Bingo—Fiction.

Classification: LCC PZ8.3.S8228 Fl 2022 | DDC [E]—dc23

LC record available at https://lccn.loc.gov/2021041115

Tonight is the night!

It is time to go.

We do not want to be late

for Flamingo Bingo!

Find a seat, Parakeet,
as the crowds overflow.

Puffin eyes prizes.

The crows want a show.

Flamingo one,
flamingo two,
flamingo three.
Hello!

BINGO
1
16
31
46
61

Crank the handle.

Balls spin.

The bingo board
will soon fill in.

O—

Oh . . . oh . . . oh . . .

Flamingo slips.

Flamingo slides.

Flamingo trips.
Flamingo rides.

The crowd gasps.
Is the game done?
But there is a card
that only needs one. . . .

A wing there,
a leg here,
feathers in a tangle.

BINGO
NIGHT

What is what
and who is who?
That is an odd angle. . . .

The crowd jumps up
and out of the way.

The flamingos roll by,
and the crows join the fray,
cawing, "Oh, what a great
show this is today!"

They slow to a crawl.

What is that popping out?

From inside the bird ball

comes a shout.

The crowd's excitement
starts to grow
as **68** is called,
and the letter **O**!

"Bravo, bravo!"
The birds all crow.

All but one
in the very last row. . . .

Toucan sits quietly
checking his card—
first the top line,
then the one below.

He opens his beak and yells,
"BINGO!"

The flamingos untangle.
The crowd settles down.
Toucan is awarded
the bingo crown.

All the birds turn to leave,

a gift bag in each wing.